The Absence of Wings

By

Mark Stewart

These stories are dedicated to the many animals that struggle to survive in the human world. May they all live to see a more compassionate age.

Acknowledgements

Grateful thanks to Robert Macfarlane for providing encouraging words of support, as well as inspiration drawn from his remarkable books.

I am indebted to Richard Hayes for his considerable editorial expertise in proofing the manuscript.

Appreciation is also extended to Sarah Stribbling for providing the wonderful cover design. More on Sarah's artwork can be found on her website: www.sarahstribblingwildlifeart.com

Lastly, I am forever grateful to one particular member of the Leporidae family of mammals, who set me on the path to writing this collection, and who inspired my first short story, *A Summer Sky*.This short story has been included in the collection in recognition of this debt, and can also be found on my website (markdestewart.wixsite.com/thescreamingplanet) and Facebook page.

Contents

A Summer Sky

For the longest time he had known only the wire mesh and the wooden walls, and the filthy straw beneath his body. Some days there was food, thrown through a door that barely opened, but mostly there was nothing, not even rotting cabbage. Long ago what little water there was had become undrinkable, having turned the colour of pond algae. In the summer, the ticks and the flies were like thorns piercing his flesh; in the winter – a time of darkness and shivering and damp – the cold drained his body of warmth. Draughts found their way through every hole and gap in the wood, nudging him awake when he wanted to sleep, covering him in a blanket of frost.

For the most part he sat in the same place, still and upright and unmoving, his body hunched. Loneliness, more piercing than the torments of summer, was his only companion. The muscles in his legs had started to atrophy, like the bones of an astronaut who has spent too long in space. At night, the only light he saw was that of the Moon; and in the day the only shade was a tarpaulin roof, hotter than the door of an oven. He began to long for release, not the freedom of the open meadow or the garden they never let him enter, but of the long sleep, the one he would never wake from, the darkness into which he would gladly have gone just to be rid of the narrow confines of the world in which he lived.

And then one day...gentle fingers closed around his body and lifted him free of the rotting straw, which still clung to him like the vines of a tropical swamp, as if each strand were reluctant to let him go. He was placed for a while in a much smaller box, a travelling case, onto the floor of which he slumped, certain that this would be his last journey. But, not long after, the same soft hands retrieved him from the box and stroked his fur, while it was cleaned and freed of the mites that had found a home there. It felt good – almost like a rebirth – to be free of the dirt that had encrusted his body for so long and for his nails, which had grown into wounding scythes, to be cut.

Tentatively, as if he couldn't quite believe it, he sniffed fresh hay and kale and began to eat. The hutch that became his new home was large and clean and dry, and there were days, many of them, when he hopped free of its walls, grass beneath his feet. He learned to run – there had never been space before – skipping and twisting in the air until he was happy and tired and ready for sleep.

Now when the rabbit sleeps, he dreams not of death but of a bright meadow to play in and clean hay to sleep on. But most of all he dreams of the warm sun and the young doe he lives with, the companion he had longed for and whose life he now shares.

Asleep and at peace, the rabbit dreams beneath a summer sky.

Dream Daemon

The big fish moved through the open water, its tightly muscled tail-fin barely flexing. The impetus for his ceaseless forward motion seemed to come from the ocean itself, as if he were drawing on a latent kinetic energy contained in the surrounding currents. He swam through immense columns of submerged sunlight, his shape both shadow and substance; occasionally he passed into less illuminated realms, slipping in and out of a submarine haze, his sinuous form now sharply defined, now a vague, smoky shadow.

Amidst such ambiguity the eye was easily deceived. Sometimes the fish seemed to have a multiplicity of fins; at other times these became a single large dorsal, like the elaborate sail on the spine of a sauropod; on yet other occasions, he displayed several smaller fins aligned in a row like the peaks of a mountain range foreshortened by distance. He seemed transfigured by the water as he moved, the focus of a strange alchemy, so that his body itself became a reflection, an image conjured from the depths. Caught in this eldritch spell, sometimes the fish was blue, sometimes black. Sometimes his belly was white, sometimes grey. Sometimes his head was shaped like an anvil or hammer, at other times he had whiskers like those of a cat. Whatever form he took, his life was always a hunted thing, pursued more remorselessly than any other creature.

*

His body was a vessel unto itself – a vessel that didn't need to be any bigger than it was. He was a thing born of a dream tide, a coalescence of the ocean, a meta-morph which took its skeleton from a fusion of mineral salts, its blood from its coldest tides, and its skin from the web of its currents. Like so many creatures he was never meant to be touched by human hands for the surface of his skin was like the edge of a blade, lacerating and wounding, a much needed way of protecting himself.

His body was a sine wave that precisely matched the harmonics of the ocean. As the serpent moves on the land, so he moved on the water, in a long lateral weave. Sentinel-like he patrolled the decks of submerged galleons, as if protecting the souls of long-drowned mariners. Or slowly climbed the circular tower of a submarine thermal, twisting into view, his supple spine a corkscrew around which his body turned. Or prowled reefs that were now a fraction of their former size and which had lost much of their colour, their vibrancy depleted as if by a sinking cloud of uranium. Or passed unseen within arm's reach of the diver and the snorkeler, a presence sensed rather than glimpsed, here and gone again, leaving behind the subcutaneous chill which signals mortal danger. In such encounters he always spared far more than he took.

He preferred to stay away from coastal shores and to hunt in the open ocean. He knew that the closer he got to land, the closer he got to the killing zone, a place of nets and harpoons. He had seen others of his kind drown in those nets, suffocating as surely as if they had been thrown onto the land. And he learnt at an early age to stay away from the surface of the water, from the baits and the hooks that waited there to snare him. His eyes could see the vague shapes that moved in that mirror world, the world on the other side of the water, where the predators lived. He could even hear their voices, muffled sounds of creatures so unlike him they might have come from another world.

He had seen other fish hauled out of the ocean, heaved onto a floating butcher's slab, their lungs removed even as they gulped for air, their eyes stabbed out even as they stared at the water they would never return to, their hearts eviscerated even as their gills pulsed like the fontanelle in the soft skull of an infant human. And finally a meat hook thrust into the cavity of their open belly, the body hoisted and hung and left to bleed out like the victim of a medieval execution, if that body wasn't already dead. It was a killing frenzy that turned the water the colour of a blood moon. He always turned away from the scraps that entered the water when the butcher's slab was swept clean, preferring hunger to tainted carrion.

And he shunned the iron clad giants, the armoured and arsenal carrying behemoths, whose rhythmic acoustical voices he found so disorientating; and shunned, too, the immense shadows that moved on the surface of the water, trailing metal nets that seemed to span the entire ocean.

Sometimes he took his prey in less than three feet of water as legend said he did, but more often it was far from the shore. It was true that he was a miracle of evolution but he did far more than just swim, eat and help to make baby sharks. As with all living things he was a thread that bound the tapestry of the biosphere together, a delicate weave that had been unravelling for decades now due to the excesses of one species. And the Mac-the-Knife grin, the predatory leer, was as misleading as the supposed smile of the dolphin; both were misperceived by so many human eyes, by a collective gaze that was only too keen to project the sentimental or the sinister onto the face of Nature.

Most of all he was a solitary wanderer, content with his companionable solitude.

He swam ever forward because evolution had designed him that way, and because such soothing compulsions were a joy to perform, not a chore. He passed through the ocean just as the ocean passed through him. Such transactions allowed him not just to breathe but to exist as he was meant to exist. And simply by existing he perpetuated a lineage older than that of almost any other creature, continuing a species bloodline that pre-dated the advent of the meteor impact which had killed his far larger ancestors – including the Megalodon – and whose ancient traces could still be found on the ocean floor, the submerged imprint of an extinction event.

*

In the end, he succumbed not to bait and line, or to hook and harpoon, but to something far more insidious and inescapable, to a cancer of his cells. To the slow death of radiation poisoning, an invisible malaise leaking into the ocean from a ruptured power plant, which sat on the coast like a malignant mechanical tumor, spreading its infection into remote places of the sea, into deep tides and submerged caverns. He never saw the hand that killed him, for those hands were many and they belonged to men who lived far from the sea, the descendants of others who had once sent armies to rape and to ravage neighboring countries. Men of martial spirit possessed by the ghosts of long dead Samurai who saw the ocean as just another commodity to be exploited if necessary to the point of total depletion.

Eventually the tides took his body onto the shore, where for a while it became an object of curiosity and disbelief, something to nudge with the toe of a boot, or to serve as an improvised ash tray where a cigarette might be snubbed out. Initials were cut into his skin along with random shapes and forms, the graffiti of the alienated and the disconnected, the dyslexic cuneiform of modern savages.

Mercifully, as if the sea itself could bear no more, the same currents soon reclaimed the dead mariner so that his brief appearance on the shoreline quickly became the stuff of rumor and legend. He sank in time to the floor of the ocean, where he dissolved into the ancient sand. Sometimes, when the tempests came, the currents even at those great depths would stir the sea bed and his shape would reform, like a phantasm glimpsed in a sandstorm, and he would swim again, the ghost of a ghost, haunting the spectral plains that lie far below the surface. A shape that would sometimes find its way into the slumbering minds of men, provoking night terrors from which some would never wake. Thus, held in the tender jaws of the dream demon, many a human soul descends into the depths never to rise again.

Long Journey Home

His nose, resting upon his folded paws, twitches as he sleeps, and his eyes move behind his folded lids, surveying a world as hidden from view as an ocean floor. He dreams the most human of dreams. A dream of hearth and home, of four walls and a sheltering roof, a house that is cool in summer and warm in winter. A house that will keep him safe no matter what storms may come. And he dreams of a kindly companion to watch over him, a provider of food and exercise whenever it's wanted.

Then, twitching still, he awakes, not from his familiar dream of sanctuary and salvation, but to an altogether different world, a world where if he dreams at all it is to dream of pursuit and escape, of the hunt and of being hunted. The rug beneath him gives way to dust and scrub grass, both coarse and grainy, the walls recede to form a distant horizon, and the fire becomes a furnace in the sky overhead, its doors flung open to bake the land beneath.

Around him in the near dark other noses are quivering, smelling the warming air, scenting its potential.

It is that eldritch hour, a reversed twilight, when the land is at its most primeval, as if it were still the realm of giant lizards whose bones have yet to turn to stone and sink into the ground to await a resurrection of sorts, a forensic disinterment, that will be millions of years in the coming.

To our eyes he appears both strange and familiar. His distinctive shape hooks our gaze and tugs it back to look again. The black ears are overlarge and the hind legs seem locked in a permanent crouch as if he is forever ready to pounce, to dart this way or that, towards danger or away from it. It is an odd posture, suggesting that he is moving even when still, the kinetic potential of his hind limbs like a primed crossbow awaiting the moment of release. For even if you are not the prey the hunt is a dangerous endeavour, a venture of hazard and chance. The slightest stumble, the merest wound, and roles are instantly reversed: the hunter becomes the hunted. Only the fit and the fearless, the cunning and the careful, survive.

But the strangeness, his essential otherness, resides most of all in the colours of his pelt, the sub-Saharan browns and muddy tans all interwoven with dark patches, every bit as black as a starless sky. They are the emblematic and totemic colours of the open savannah.

He has the sad contemplative eyes of an Alsatian but his teeth belong more rightly in the jaws of the wolf. His appearance might well confound those who are governed by a schoolboy obsession with classification, phylogeny and morphology. Where does he belong in the cabinet of scientific curiosities? For he is neither leopard nor hyena but yet has shades of both; he is canine and yet not canine, assembled from an earlier, more atavistic pattern, roughhewn as if he remains a draft or sketch of what was to come later, a biological prototype.

He possesses the fearsome demeanour and focussed intent of all the hyper-carnivorous, of those who must eat meat on a daily basis in order to survive. In the chase and the kill, its ways are brutal and savage but less so than the horrors that take place in the abattoir and on the factory farm.

In truth he is terrified of his companions, even though they are kith and kin. He is a soul born into the wrong body. He has learnt how to hide his otherness, to keep it under his skin the way a man might conceal his wallet. He must dissemble and deceive, hiding his fear away, knowing that it is the most distinctive of all pheromones, and that once detected it would be the end of him. The pack would turn on the stranger, the interloper in their midst, as surely as if he had broken a leg or been fatally wounded in a skirmish or a hunt.

Perhaps it is fair to say that he has more honour than the hyena, who is happy to steal the kills made by other predators. Each of their hunts is a tempest and he gives himself willingly to the storm, letting it carry him along to its inevitable bloody conclusion. None of the others notice his reluctance, if reluctance it is. So he conceals himself in plain sight, using the painted colours of his skin to hide and not to hide, indistinguishable from his canid companions, as much a member of this small ferocious fraternity as any of the others. But there is tenderness in the savagery too, for meals are often regurgitated for the pups and for other adults. And they seldom turn on their own kind, having a sufficiency of enemies in the lion and the human. Of the two, the two legged predator is by far the more rapacious, killing from a wanton appetite that has nothing to do with sating a hunger for food.

To our sentimental, discriminating hearts he would be a hard creature to love. But then he might say the same, and worse, of us. And with good reason. Nature may be red in tooth and claw but the ways of men are redder still. Like the buffalo his kind have been hunted almost to extinction. Shot and skinned and fashioned into cairns of white bone bleached by the sun.

*

His is a dry world, a world of dust and sand and scrub, into which he can blend as if moving through the night in a coat of shadows, moving as seamlessly as the leopard. In his desert coat he will hunt because it is in his nature to do so, because he must hunt or perish. But he is seldom the one who brings down the wildebeest, the springbok, or the warthog, least of all the warthog with its sabre toothed jaw and eviscerating tusks. And he is more frightened still of the lion and the human both of whom would gladly make a trophy of his bones. He knows the savagery of the human is of a different order to anything else that hunts and kills on the open plain. It is a savagery that has pushed his kind to the brink of extinction, to the edge of the evolutionary chasm from which none can re-emerge. His pack lives and sleeps on the edge of the abyss, on the edge of the all-devouring precipice that still threatens to consume them all.

As yet, he is too small to fight for a female companion and so he lives a solitary life within the pack. But he knows this will change for already he can feel the muscles thickening in his limbs and his jaw becoming dense with sinew and bone as he grows into his body, gradually inhabiting its potential like the fingers of a hand pushing their way into a gauntlet; but for now he must bide his time. And he has a companion of sorts to assuage his loneliness, a spectral presence that keeps him company in the long watches of the night when such company is most needed.

He moves as close as he can to the Moon whenever it rises into the black sky, seeking out the brightest patch of silver light and sitting in the moon-glow, eyes upcast, entranced by a world that always seems much closer than it really is. He has no way of knowing, and perhaps could not have understood, that others of his kind had once ventured to the very fringes of space, taking the first steps on a path that would eventually lead to the Moon, fired into space in aluminium capsules to see if it was safe for humans to follow. Few had survived those expeditions, regardless of what the propaganda agencies had claimed, their sacrifice undone when that lofty destination had been abandoned by the last of the lunar mariners.

He searched for the Moon's reflection in the watering holes he visited. But, like the scattered constellations that also caught the attention of his upturned gaze, the pale chimera was never to be seen during the day. And to him the stars were like a rain shower that never fell, as if the ebon sky itself had frozen over.

Thus, at night when the sun disappears so comprehensively it is hard to believe it ever existed, his one source of solace is its luminescent cousin, the one whose dusty light contains no warmth at all. He spends hours watching this penumbral sun shining in the liquid blackness, fascinated by its eldritch and hieratic glow, by a febrile reflection that seems more tenuous than the smoke of a wood fire. Perhaps his eyes are sharp enough to see the mountains of the Moon, to see the rimmed craters filled with the ancient dust of meteorites and comets. And perhaps he wonders what it might be like to wander there, to sniff the trails and tracks of the cold, silver sun, to explore a land where the dust beneath his feet might record his footprints and his alone. For often there is a look in his eyes that says he has indeed been there, that he has walked over the sky to the Moon, and longs to go back if only he can remember the way; he has the eyes of a stargazer, a regard habitually fixed on distant destinations.

*

The lion came at him as if he'd used the savannah as a cloak, concealing himself behind invisible corners formed by the wind and the sky, from the hidden intersections that always favour the hunter over his quarry. From these elemental geometries he fell upon the smaller carnivore, as the harrier falls upon the mouse, and from almost an equal height. From the outset it was an uneven contest. The larger beast simply had more of everything: more ferocity and tenacity, more determination and guile. He came from the long shadows cast by the unflinching sun, a penumbral predator that quickly wrapped itself in a murderous intent.

He felt the lion's weight upon him and his hot breath. It was as though the very sun itself had collapsed upon his back, its great mass bearing down, its furnace breath hotter than anything he had ever known. With insolent ease the lion opened the flanks of its prey – inflicting long, piercing tears that spoke more eloquently of the impending doom than a funeral bell tolling in its tower – and delved inside as if plucking at a tray of sweet meats.

It was as if the lion were intent upon unmaking him, unrobing him by the cut and thrust of his claws, dispossessing him first of his skin and then of the very meat on his bones. As a tailor might have measured him for his close fitting pelt, so the lion unmeasured him, leaving him bereft of all substance save that of cartilage, spleen and marrow. Long before this process was complete the lion's quarry had departed that same thin organic envelope, folding himself away as if in preparation for an upcoming journey. As sudden as the transition was, almost as quick as a blade falling onto a headman's block, he knew where he was going, perhaps more so than the canine and primate voyagers who had once travelled atop those primitive rockets, exchanging one universe for another, much as he was doing now.

He slipped between the physical and the metaphysical using the same devices that the lion had only moments before. The transition was a tiring one and when at last he arrived at his new but familiar destination he collapsed in front of the well-lit hearth, content just to lie still and catch his breath and to put some warmth back into his limbs. In time, his companion laid a bowl of water and another of food not far from the rug on which he lay, and patted his flank in welcome.

Home at last, the small dog slept beside the fire, his nose twitching on his folded paws.

Prisoner of the Carnival Arcade

Even in the womb he dreams of the savannah, of the journeys he will make across the open plain, his paws clenching at the thought of treading grass and sand, of touching the same earth that other creatures have walked upon. Snug inside the floating womb, the cradle which seems to gently rock even when his mother is still, he yearns for the big sky, the furnace sky – a sky big enough to hold other suns and their attendant worlds – that mirrors the plains, for the endless horizons his new home will bring him. And he longs for the jungle that exists at the far edge of those plains, a jungle so old that sauropod footprints might still be found in its moist clays.

Even through his mother's skin he can already feel the heat of the grasslands, rousing his instincts, burning in his blood. His heartbeat quickens and his eyelids flicker as he searches for gazelle and antelope, his nose twitching to find their scent on the hot air. The buffalo of his dreams seems huge to his unopened eyes, too big ever to bring down. But when the time comes, he slips from his mother's body not onto the soft and welcoming floor of his ancestral home but onto cold concrete.

*

There are iron bars where his horizon should be and that horizon is only a few feet away. He paces and pads and prowls but cannot wear down by sheer force of will the bars that keep him from freedom, from the liberty that is his birth right. He patrols the borders of his cage with all the diligence of a sentry but still cannot find a single opening through which he might escape. He cannot know that there is nowhere to escape to, that he is surrounded by roads rather than rivers, and by electricity pylons rather than by trees. He cannot know that, even had he jumped those walls, all that waited for him on the other side was a lonely death in the corner of a derelict field; a bullet from a marksman's rifle bringing the hunt to an end. His life and death would be worth no more than a momentary update on the evening news: an impromptu Home Counties safari that ends with a picture of a delighted hunter, most probably a police marksman, with his foot resting on the head of an unexpected trophy.

He *wants* to hunt, and searches endlessly for his quarry, but he cannot give chase for there is nothing to chase. The watering hole around which he should have gathered with the rest of the pride is little more than a muddy sump in the ground; the water is only ever replaced when it rains, which it does often in this sullen country, far from his sub-Saharan home. The prairie should be as limitless for him as the ocean is for the whale; but he is hemmed in, forever constrained, by walls of glass and plastic and there is nothing but concrete where the wildness should be.

Falling upon his ears, as he lies in tree shade recovering from the hunt, should come the metallic murmur of insects and the sound of the ground cooking in the heat, the buzz of baked earth and tinder-dry grass, like the hum of electricity through telegraph lines. Instead he must contend with an incessant cacophony, a vulgar chorus emanating from the theme park, the screams and the shouts, and the endless throbbing music.

His coat has grown pale in the cold; unlike his cousin, he will never be the luminescent being of legend, burning brightly in the forests of the night, for the fire has left his soul, snuffed out by long years of imprisonment. He knows now that he will never see the land he dreamt of in the womb.

His captors imagine him to be lethargic and lazy but in truth his jailers have stolen away his vigour and his vitality. He sleeps because sleep is his only escape; asleep he can dream of the hunt he will never go on, of the prey he will never bring down. He has barely enough energy to power a slow stumbling gait. His muscles, engines of sinew and cartilage that should have driven countless pursuits, have atrophied, wasting away just as paper turns to dust, as even the greatest conflagrations turn to ash. His life is a book which consists of blank pages each as colourless as an overcast sky, a sky more sombre than a funeral cortege. Above all, it is solitude that has doused the candle of his spirit.

The breeze, which should have brought him primeval scents, is redolent with the stink of burnt meat and the over-ripe aromas of candy floss, beer and chips. And everywhere there is the smell of humans: excremental and over-powering. The air should have been thick with the multifoliate aromas of forest and jungle, each scent as clearly defined as footsteps in a lunar plain. Instead his olfactory senses have been dulled and corrupted, like a long-forgotten blade corroded by the very soil it has been lost in.

His hunting grounds have been tarmacked over to make way for a car park, covered with concrete to provide the foundations for a hotel, and divided into endless plots for theme park attractions. He sits in the middle of all this in a space most humans would have considered too small for a garden. He is starved intermittently in an effort to replicate those days in the wild on which he might not have made a kill; but in truth such deprivations are an attempt to stave off the obesity that goes with a sedentary life. He longs not to be fed but to hunt, to find his own meat, not to have it brought to him on a hook and thrown into his cage as a fisherman might bait and cast a line. Captivity has reduced him from a king to the status of a pauper feeding from a metal bowl.

His gaze has long ago turned inward, away from the invasive eyes that peer at him relentlessly from beyond the glass walls, the peeping Tom intrusions that are a continual reminder of the privacy he lacks. He longs for the sight of other creatures, for the companionable sight of elephant and giraffe, shapes that have morphed into gaudy caricatures in the rides that take place beyond his prison walls. His eyes search in vain for the other worldly forms that only Africa can summon into being, creatures that might have seemed unlikely even in the dreams of an exo-biologist.

He has suffered a multiplicity of thefts, the worst being the loss of his voice, a voice that should have rattled the very windows through which his tormentors gawp at him. And hourly it should have shaken, like a bomb blast, the windows in every house for miles around. But the blood of his keepers remains unchilled by such detonations, for they never happen; the silence within his enclosure remains unbroken, his voice a pale flag fluttering in an empty breeze.

Paws that should have felled a buffalo with a single swipe now swat at nothing more than the occasional fly. This is evolution operating in reverse, a slow insidious cancer of the genes. There is no dignity in his captivity (how could there be?) for he is now no more than an exhibit in a carnival arcade. He hears daily the sound of gunfire from the nearby shooting gallery and longs for the fairground players to turn their fire in his direction, if only for the respite it would bring from loneliness, from the agonies of the wound that never heals.

In the end his life simply ebbs away, like a retreating tide that never returns. He lies down in his bare sleeping den and never gets up again. Like any proud monarch he should have died in battle, fighting for his kingdom; but his dominion was taken from him the moment he was born. On the day that he dies the gates to the theme park are open as usual but his enclosure remains empty. There are grumbles and complaints about the lack of an occupant but the protests don't last long. For, not far away, the cages are full of other captives, all of whom once dreamed of freedom in their mother's womb.

The Absence of Wings

He was born in the season of Spring tides and cherry blossom, and his first memory was of the warmth of his mother's fur as he lay high up in the tree hollow, his face pressed into the soft down of her belly. Once he ventured outside, he bonded quickly with his avian cousins. Indeed, for a while, he thought of himself as a bird, believing it was only a matter of time before he would be able to fly. Only slowly did he notice the absence of wings amongst his own limbs, and by then he was already as quick and as fleet as the tiny birds that seemed to teleport from one location to another, so fast was their transition from bough to bough. For by then he had found the arboreal web linking tree to tree, across which he moved like a miniature Greystoke among the vines of ivy.

The same eyes that were quick to see him as a pest failed to notice his white belly as bright as the pelage of the snow hare; or the smoky golden burr that ran down his back and into his tail, as iridescent as the hide of a silverback gorilla. And the hands that were so inventive in constructing ways in which he might be killed never reached out in kindness with food. All except one. He knew he would not have survived for long – especially in the thin season when the sun seemed to withdraw much of its light – without the human who threw nuts and berries onto her lawn each morning. On occasion he even took one of these gifts from her hand. But he never forgot that she was the exception. It was still (and always would be) safest to spurn the ragged, sullen tatterdemalions who claimed total dominion of field and forest, right down to the last scrap of derelict land, to avoid "the walking heads of men." These ambulant scarecrows reeked of the grave, of dead things hung upon a gibbet, the stink as palpable as wood smoke; they knew only how to tramp and to trammel the ground as they blundered through field and forest, garden and park.

"Vermin!" "Pox carrier!" Their guttural language, most often expressed in shouts and curses, was alien to him but he understood those words well enough: they meant death by poison, by stoning, by pellets fired from air guns, and worst of all by the lingering torment of the snare, the inescapable piercing wire – more lacerating than the sharpest thorn – that he feared most of all. So he ran,

running to stay alive, following branch and bough, just so he could carry on breathing.

And he understood what we do not, that all the many trees are one, that every branch and bough is a ley-line, a path through the lower reaches of the sky that no human could follow, every limb an outstretched arm offering him a new escape route. *Hurry! This way! Quick as you can!* He knew that each trunk, no matter how insubstantial, was an open portal providing access to an infinite forest, a sanctuary for all hunted creatures. And for a while he managed to out-run his many enemies. He even learnt how to survive the death of summer and the onset of winter, to evade the Long Darkness and the broad sweep of its heavy penumbral cloak, beneath which so many vanished never to re-emerge. And he might have gone on running from tree to tree had it not been for the oddly coloured pellets he found scattered on the ground in an adjoining garden. Their colour should have been warning enough but he was so hungry that he ate several nonetheless. He made it into the tree canopy before the stomach cramps started.

He died in the season of the winter solstice, not having lived long enough to find a companion with whom he might have raised a family. His last sensation was that of the cold earth pressing up on his body, the clay already exerting a claim on his very substance that he could not refute. Above him, the One Tree cast a fading image upon his retinas, the light receding from his eyes as his final breath, the merest susurration, slipped from his lungs.

*

The woman found his body not long after. Gently she laid a hand upon his fur to satisfy herself that it no longer held any warmth, and then she carried the tiny form – hardly bigger than her palm – beneath the overhanging boughs of the nearby Yew tree. The stiffness of the body – and the rictus that had distorted the shape of the creature's mouth – told her how he had died, that he had succumbed to the poison laid by one of her neighbours. It was the work of only a few minutes to trowel out the small grave. Before she covered the body with a piece of cloth she laid two berries close to the creature's head, as if providing provisions for an afterlife. Then she smoothed over the earth and stood beside the grave, conscious that the newly dead still often need the company of the living. She glanced up at the tree canopy aware that such arteries belonged as much to the sky as the ground, that the canopies were rooted in the air as much as they were in the soil, their bark-covered filaments providing a perch for bird and squirrel alike.

The boughs moved quietly in the wind, whispering their marine song like lonely sirens, as she walked back to her kitchen, scattering berries and nuts as she crossed the empty lawn. Behind her the cherry tree stood gaunt and bare, its blossoms belonging now to a different season.

The Crocodile's Tears

Its body is a dense fabric of overlapping armour plates, save for the soft white underbelly, a vulnerability so piercing that it is almost too much to look upon. Its unblinking eyes are emerald jewels, glinting with cognisance. Its tail is its most powerful limb, stronger by far than the short legs or the webbed and padded feet. Its long jaws, from prow to stern, are the jaws of the Iron Maiden; it possesses a fatal embrace which once conferred is inescapable. It is an engine of muscle and sinew, tightly coiled, as full of deadly potential as the cocked hammer on a gun. Its armour is inviolate and impenetrable, and once engaged the attentions of the warrior that lives inside this armour are undeniable. It is the last of the dragons and its days are nearly done.

It is a creature misplaced in time. It belongs more rightly on a different world, a tropical world of lavish foliage, a world which exists in greater proximity to its star. When we view the creature now, we see a dusty savannah and a dull, placid river in which the creature swims, as a captive lion might prowl behind the bars of its too-small cell.

Were you to stand behind the windows of its eyes you would see a very different landscape, a domain that no human eyes have ever witnessed first-hand. This is the world of a luxuriant garden pond grown to tropical excess, a pond that has become a lake, a lake that has become an inland sea with tides and currents all of its own. There are ferns that would dwarf the great Victorian hothouses at Kew, overtopping the glass roofs like the distended arms of a giant triffid; there are glimmering, electric dragonflies the size of seagulls, and gulls the size of pterodactyls. There are ground nesting lizards whose eggs – elongated spheres the size and shape of rugby balls – only the foolhardy or the desperate would try to steal. There is a cat with the tusks of a mammoth and an elephant with the dusty pelt of a bear. This metamorphic pond has spawned lily pads the size of cricket pitches, and infant amphibians the size of fully grown trout. In the shallows of the pond are immense, golden salamanders and heraldic frogs the size of canines. Skating the surface are insects with skeletal limbs and antennae big enough, and sturdy enough, to capsize a canoe and to deal unhesitatingly with its occupants.

The lake is fed by rivers wider and warmer and deeper than the Thames has ever been, or will ever be, whose shores are home to reptilian footprints which, once excavated and transported, will one day become the prize exhibit in museum halls, in cathedrals devoted to the celebration of extinction. The air above this Cretaceous pond is thick and heavy, pressing down from a sky illuminated by a young sun. It is a sky that sucks moisture from the air, only to return it again as a sizzling tepid rain. The world will never again be so alive, so populated, so densely wrapped in a mantle of living things. After the next extinction event, a doom which is already hurtling through space towards this unsuspecting world, the Earth will only ever be tame by comparison.

And just below the surface of this lake-sized pond, like a newt grown to gargantuan proportions, floats a creature that is neither dragon nor serpent but somehow both. He is an innocent shaman, a disguiser of his true colours; he hides behind subtle deceptions: now a floating log, now just a patch of surface weed. But one thing that never changes are jaws that clamp and bind with irreversible finality. He has the jaws of the most terrible of all the primordial lizards and the patience of a cetacean. He will spin the bodies of his submerged prey as if upon the loom of a spider's web, stocking his larder so that he need not eat again for days to come.

There is not a scrap of humanity about him and he is all the better for it. He is often overlooked by those who search for lost worlds. This is the country of Bradbury, Burroughs and Doyle, long before that land was usurped by latter day movie moguls interested only in ticket sales and derivative re-imaginings.

He is wrapped in the skin of the tyrannosaurus, a pebbly epidermis that resembles tree bark or the knobbly coat of a goblin, all hives and pocks. And yet it is a thing of fearsome beauty, like the spiked mantle of a stegosaurus, or the white, woven stiletto of the unicorn. He is the river wolf, even though he is a solitary hunter. His howl is a hissing roar, as though he possesses a serpent's tongue. To hear that voice is to know that you have stepped into a circle of doom, to know that your fate is as sealed as the jaws that will soon be grinding your bones deep below the surface of the river in a submarine cave already full to the brim with rattling revenants. The gun has been cocked and now the hammer is about to fall. And yet, for all that, he is not a wanton killer; there is no trace of gluttony about his hunger; his dispatches fall within the realm of moderation; he takes only what he needs to live.

On the land he knows he is vulnerable so he seldom strays far from the edge of the lake. Once in the water he is all but invincible, though he knows well enough to leave alone the hippo and the giant boa.

He does not live in the river; the river lives within him. For him the water is a dimension of being; he is more closely related to its substance than he is to any other animal. He may draw his air when he surfaces, filling his lungs as a submersible fills its oxygen tanks, but he breathes *through* the water. The river is the limb that cannot be seen, that cannot be dissevered from the rest of his body, even in death. It is a source of potency stronger than his jaws or tail, and it renders him invulnerable to all but one enemy.

As with the shark and the turtle his age is unguessable. He has accumulated more than enough years to be treated with respect, to be venerated.

His status as a member of an Elder Species should have afforded him absolute protection. Few voices in the council of living things should have been more revered. But he is watched by eyes that take no notice of his existence, that see him only in terms of the ledger book and the balance sheet, that confer upon him no right to a dignified life, or indeed any form of life at all. He is watched in other words by human eyes. Watched and appraised and evaluated and found to be worth more dead than alive.

Human eyes see only the low slung beast of nursery tales, the plodding Peter Pan villain with the sinister, elongated smile. Such a regard holds him to be little better than a serpent; it fails to recognise his more ancient and abiding claim upon the Earth, a right to exist which pre-dates homo sapiens by millennia. In the great book of life he appears long before the upright ape but it is the tool-wielding ape that has whittled down the book of life so savagely, reducing the register of all things extant as if this wilful holocaust were a virtue.

*

Its younger self was absurdly small, more vulnerable than a baby turtle. It knew danger then and fear, and many of its kind grew little bigger before being snatched from the water by beak or by talon. But grow it did and over time it shed its fear like a second skin. Just as the lion is king on the land so it ruled the waterways and the lakes.

Now, once again, it is a size that we would recognise as proportionate and appropriate but it still looks atavistically alien, out of place in an increasingly tame world. Like the wolf and the hyena, the shark and the bear, it has been forced to play the role of villain by the one creature more perfectly suited to that caricature than any other. It kills not so it can own the hide of another animal, fashioned into a handbag or a pair of boots, its skin used as human tissue was once used to create lampshades; nor does it kill for pleasure. It hunts simply so it can go on living from one day to the next.

That succession of days, a tally that should have seen it live to seventy years of age or more, is brought to an abrupt end by the hunter's bullet. It is dead long before it is hauled from the water, its body flipped by the toe of a boot, and its belly cut open.

The sniper's bullet is an obscenity, the projectile somehow pornographic, revealing a violent penetration that should never have happened. The creature's demise is indecently quick, especially in a land ruled by the slower rhythms of sunrise and sunset, and all that falls between. The hasty death will be followed by an equally abrupt dismemberment for the fashionistas are keen to display their vulgarity, to parade themselves for the cameras in the skin of another animal.

His heart, a thing of savage but profound beauty, like a rose of the wild wood, disintegrates the moment the bullet strikes. In the same instant, the twin suns that inhabit his eyes expire, dowsed like candles. All trace of energy and vitality departs from his body, which becomes as limp as a kite crushed by the wind.

As for the heart of the hunter: there is an empty vortex, the deepest of black holes, where that biological mechanism should be, and an automated system of repeating cogs and gears where the cerebellum should reside. He is a simulacrum, an imitation human, bereft of empathy.

If you have tears prepare to shed them now, not for the Bard's haughty Moor who loved not wisely but too well, but for the last of these creatures. There are too few now for their kind to survive. Their species has reached the final tipping point and the chasm of extinction, a bottomless pit of nullity, looms before them. Into this abyss they will be herded by a creature that is entirely responsible for the last of all the Earth's great extinction events.

*

In another age, long ago, the great aquatic lizard swims on, undisturbed and unmolested. When the giant meteor comes – the re-shaper of worlds – it will simply ride out the ensuing firestorm, resurfacing aeons later on the continent that will come to be known as Africa, where its eyes will survey a different more barren land, until its gaze turns inwards and it recalls the land of an earlier Earth, a place where it was free from persecution. In a land that time forgot, before humans walked the Earth.

The Empty Ocean

It was made of sea spray and salt mist and white caps, of sea beams and moon-lit shadows that ripple on the surface of the ocean far from shore. It was made of siren-song, of the soft lilting murmurings of mermaids and their children pining for husbands and fathers to return from the sea. It was made of sea grass and kelp, and sunlight that had coalesced in the oceans depths into something composed of more than just photons: the crystallisation of tides and currents into flesh and blood.

Its hide, which was both mirror and abyss, was as smooth as a glacier or a wave-worn pebble, a pebble the size of a berg, a berg that had been carved and shaped on Olympus and dropped into the ocean to make others of its kind. It was an ocean going Will-o'-the-wisp, phantasmagorical and transcendent, yet real enough to leave a wake that no ship could match in size or depth. Its passage through the ocean was a frictionless glide, moving with the ease of a god stretching out its hand. It moved through the water the way a raptor soars through the air, and by comparison to which our greatest feats of ocean-going propulsion are crude and primitive.

It was a sea shanty made real, a maritime myth so believable that it had to exist, a creature that had sung itself into being. It was the biggest of big fish and yet it was not a fish at all.

It lived at depths that would crush the twin hulls of a submarine, often exchanging these remote fathoms for the upper fringes of the ocean, surfacing at the margin between atmosphere and water, where the air might warm its body like sunlight falling on the side of a mountain.

Its saurian cries, mournful bellows sadder than any lament, seemed to echo from an ancient chasm, from a well of deep-time, resonating from an age long before the first human footprints were washed away by the tide. The long song-lines, spun from vocal chambers that resonate in the spectral abyss, reach from one continental shoreline to another, through the inter-coastal depths, like radio signals that span interplanetary gulfs. They are vibrating submarine cords, telegraph lines that hum with a language we will never understand.

With a brain many times the size of our own it is anything but primitive. And what thoughts arise in the chambers and vaults of that brain concerning human behaviour? How does it view its tormentors? If we had shown more compassion and forbearance what might we have learned from minds immeasurably superior to our own?

Its jaws are benign for they seek only to sweep up the microscopic krill that it feeds on. It is a harmless giant, not the boat-crushing killer of myth and legend, the dark denizen of Ahab's nightmares.

Its colours are every shade of aquamarine, from polar white to midnight blue. Thus for all its size it can often move unseen, camouflaged by current and tide. Inseparable from those same currents and tides its sensorium reaches out into the depths, an echo sounding mesh cast wider than any human net could ever travel, probing the far fathoms with a sentience greater than our own. It is afraid only of the shadows that move on the surface of the water, for those shadows are the only thing, save for an immense accumulation of years, that can kill it.

Into this sensorium came the big boat, its funnels casting columns of smoke upon the air, its great corkscrew hacking and chopping at the water – the anvil hammered blades churning the sea, atomising the waves just as a rocket engine vaporises the air – its iron hull like the ramparts of a siege castle. And with it came the stink of harbour filth and a wake filled with empty plastic bottles, beer cans and human waste.

A leviathan in its own right, a harvester and decimator of the seas, the big boat gave chase, readying its hydraulic powered harpoons and its steel nets. The harpoon which ensnared him was pitifully small, like a javelin cast against a cliff face. But a thousand smaller barbs detonated on impact and their embrace was inescapable, like the closing of a coffin lid.

In the measurement of all things, one to the other, it should not have been possible to extract a creature of such size from the ocean; but generations of toil and practice had taught the hunters how best to capture and handle their prey. So they hauled and they heaved, lifting with pulley and with crane, with motors and with engines, drawing the creature tail first onto the killing floor, so that

49

it faced the ocean it would never again inhabit. Its final sight was an image of the gulls that wheeled about the boat, waiting for the scraps that would slip or be thrown from the cold metal decks, for the pieces of its own body that would soon stain the sea, turning it the colour of a blood moon.

While it still drew breath, they cut the living berg as men might once have reaped a field of barley, each scything stroke wielded by the hands of a ripper, each cut delivered with all the tenderness of a back street abortionist. Parts of the creature's anatomy which should never have been exposed to sunlight were opened to its most probing regard. Had it possessed the power to look away, to withdraw its light, the sun might have flinched at such intimacies. But it knew well the obscenities of man and its unflinching gaze remained steadfast and true, as resolute as the blades that quickly dismembered the largest creature on the planet. When the cutting and hacking and slicing were over, and the harvest safely stowed for conversion to cash later on in the squabbling and bartering that would take place in dockside markets, all that remained on deck were a dozen buckets of offal, ready to be cast as bait upon the waters, or simply to be thrown overboard as waste. It was as if the great beast had simply melted away, vanishing like an ocean fog, leaving only a thin mist of sea spray to mark its passing.

*

The fishing boat had set out at first light and was now far from shore. It had taken hours to lay out the chum line, which stretched for hundreds of meters like a trail of rotting bait, which is exactly what it was.

"Man! No matter how many times I do this I can never get used to the smell," said one of the deck hands, who had been tasked with laying the chum line.

"It's a stinker alright," agreed his companion. He hacked phlegm into the back of his throat and spat into the sea. "Every bad smell rolled up into one."

The first man nodded towards the cabin where those who had paid for the charter still waited for the day's sport to begin, fortifying themselves with champagne. "They should come down here and shovel some of this shit."

But though they persevered for many hours, casting line after line into the sea, the day's sport proved to be a disappointment. The sun moved round the sky, lowering its light as it went, before it too gave up the hunt. The fishermen came home with their nets empty and their hooks bare, their bait untaken. For, in the empty ocean, there was nothing left to kill.

The Moon Fish

The long blue fish swam back and forth behind the submerged bars, gazing at the open ocean beyond the wire mesh. His black coalescent eyes contained an unmistakable sentience, a gaze of infinite clarity as precise and unwavering as the targeting beam on a marksman's rifle. And right now that gaze was aimed at the only place the blue fish wanted to be.

His sight never left the depths that had once been his home, the vastness that called to him as if a choir of sirens were beckoning to him on the other side of the mesh, from the upturned keels of a thousand wrecks, from a graveyard of capsized galleons. It was a chorus, a spectral emulation of the sea's own voice, which consisted of witching, necromantic songs cast like nets upon the water to catch the unwary or the unwise. Their song was the only thing that eased the pain of his confinement, like a balm on an open wound.

*

The water in his cage had become polluted long ago, fouled by rotting scraps of meat, and by every type of harbour detritus: plastic bottles and food wrappings, a surface smear of marine oil and petrol, by thick cords of rope and discarded fishing lines, a poisonous web that was almost impossible to avoid. The fish moved with a monotonous weaving motion, searching for a flaw in the mesh, his gaze where he longed to be and where he feared he might never be again. He moved as the polar bear moves in his cage, pacing back and forth; as the tiger does in his cell, pacing from side to side; as the lion does in his prison, pacing, prowling, padding behind iron bars, all unable to answer the call of the wild.

One by one they had taken his companions; some had been re-caught in nets, others harpooned for their meat and for their oils and for their fins. He alone remained. And for all he knew, he was the last of his kind anywhere.

*

His world had never been sharp edged. From his first moment he had known only the open embrace of the sea; he had slipped from his mother's belly into this greater womb, into a smooth amniotic ocean, as boundless as the universe itself.

And from the first, even as an infant, his body had been an undulating hollow packed with muscle, a sinuous spring perpetually coiling and releasing, a frictionless motor propelling him through the water. He was born with the knowledge that we have long forgotten: he knew that the ocean is a single wave, constantly on the cusp of breaking, a continuous eternal harmonic that he rode endlessly, using its kinetic energy to hunt and to play. Above all, he loved to play in the huge shafts of sunlight that struck through the ocean on cloudless days, boring into the depths like meteor trails, creating immense columns of sheltering warmth, and illuminating the submarine world all the way to the ocean floor. As he did with the One Wave, he drew energy from these prisms of starlight, from these cosmic thermals. For like us he too was made of star-stuff.

And the oceanic light had always been filled with music, by the plaintive and hypnotic call of the deep-water sauropods – muffled sonorations like the turn of a tide in a half drowned cave – by the harmonies of the tides, more entrancing than the sweetest siren song. And by the sonic chatter of his own kind. All of these sounds were interspersed with the music of silence, with the quiet hush of deep water infinities.

He lived without fear, unafraid even of the big fish with the white belly, or its even bigger cousins that hunted in packs. He knew he could outrace them all, that for him the ocean would always be an open door through which he might escape any peril. He was an arrow head always in flight, as swift and fleet as a falling star. He lived in a liquid sky, in a mirror world where his image flashed and was gone almost before it could be seen.

His world had never been sharp edged until the day the nets found him.

*

He waited for the lunar tide to fill the harbour, for the Moon to draw breath so that he in turn might breathe again. He needed as much depth as that cold and dusty world could provide, well aware of the danger posed by the cutting wire that had been place on top of the mesh. The Moon pushed at the water and he began to circle the cage, swimming faster, riding the One Wave. He circled as the hawk circles, racing his fleeing shadow until all his strength had gathered in his tail. Then, as if mirroring the flight of Neptune's trident loosed in anger, he turned and ran straight for the mesh, uncoiling his submerged wings at the last moment.

For an instant his tail flashed beneath the surface of the sea, like the bright flukes of the sea-maidens whose songs had done so much to assuage his sadness. Flashed like mirrors filled with sunlight, as if he meant to signal his intent to the waiting sirens.

Moonbeams caught the energising vane as he rose out of the water and up over the mesh. The wire cut his pale belly, inflicting a caesarean wound, as he passed over its uppermost reach but the pain was lost in the exultation of being free. He slipped through the door to the ocean's depths and was gone before the ripples had faded on the water's surface. Out into the welcoming ocean, back into a world that was soft edged and filled with great chasms of sunlight. Hurried on by moonlight, the blue fish swam back into a world where men with nets and harpoons would never find him.

The Sea Wraith

The obsidian gloom and the cold are both so extreme, by human standards, that they seem to have fused into a single element, a medium of both temperature and darkness, almost a new dimension, through which the creature moves as silently as falling snow. As swift as a javelin passing through air it generates almost no friction, splicing through the water. It should be otherwise; its mass and shape should slow it down. But they do not. It has learnt how to propel itself, to fall upon its prey with speed and precision. It slips between the currents, passing through doors that only it knows how to open. It moves to the beat of a silent drum, pulsing through the water.

From out of the penumbral darkness, the tendrils appear first, reaching, searching, a multitude of outstretched arms, feeling the face of the water. Then comes the cone-shaped body like the housing on a jet engine, and perched on either side of this soft carapace are the great saucer-like eyes. The eyes are so vast they seem to drown their prey in a separate ocean. They are the eyes of a nocturnal creature, a mesmerizing regard that becomes sharper still the deeper those eyes go. The drowned and the damned alike are pulled and dragged by the long limbs into the beak that sits at the front of the cone, a beak larger than the leathery mandibles of a pelican, harder than the tusk of a rhino. A beak sharp enough to gut a man from his throat to his groin with a single, almost careless inflection.

It is a thing of both beauty and terror, a creature more implausible than impossible. It shouldn't exist at such depths and such pressures; nothing organic should. And yet it does. Somewhere in its blood stream, buried deep in the cells of its body, is the secret to building submersibles that can go deeper for longer. But such secrets are unlikely to fall within the narrow boundaries of human cognizance, for the great storehouses of the ocean are heading towards depletion.

It is a thing only dimly glimpsed (if glimpsed at all) in the oceans of the night, a pale spectre, a phantasm that carries its own light, wielding a lantern of bioluminescence. In the lonely watches of the night the lantern bearer might be glimpsed as it descends to ever greater depths, uncoiling into the lowest fathoms as if upon an invisible thread, more arachnid than cephalopod.

A beachcomber might search for a thousand years and find no trace or relic of the creature; not so much as a fragment of a tentacle, a single tooth, or even a flake of its marble coloured skin. It is a creature that has never seen the margins of the ocean; the foreshore is so far removed from where it lives, it might as well belong to a different planet. It has no cave or lair to hide in while it waits out the interval between hunts but rather inhabits the very interstices of the tides, its interdimensional folds and creases, from which it can fall upon its prey with all the deadly intent of a raptor.

Its flesh seems bleached of colour, like a plant that has never seen the light, a submarine triffid that has escaped its roots and is free at last to roam the ocean's deepest recesses, its further corners. As old as the Coelacanth and just as rare, evading net and line and hook alike. Some say it cannot be caught, even by the long-lined harpoons of the whaling boats, the great plunderers and despoilers of the sea. It is as elusive as the unicorn, a creature yet more terrible than anything Ahab ever dreamed of. A half formed creature, part fish, part mollusc and yet neither. It has somehow slipped free of its skeleton, if indeed it ever had one.

White tendrils as pale as the limbs of a corpse, as pale and translucent as the undead flesh of a Carpathian Countess. Deadly ribbons, each equipped with a parallel row of suckers, each sucker equipped with a circle of teeth. Thus each ribbon is doubly lethal. The tips flutter at their extremities, as if performing an arcane spell by which it might find its next meal. Or perhaps it is simply finding its way through the dark corridors of the oceanic depths, navigating and traversing the oceans by means of a chart which only it can see.

The creature more properly belongs in the tideways of space, free of Newtonian constraints, where its tendrils can span interplanetary gulfs, trapping satellites in its immense web of filaments, like damsel flies in a cosmic mesh. It is as if the darkness and the pressure have collapsed to form not a black hole but a creature that might dwell on the very cusp of such a transfiguring singularity. An analogue of such a spectral intangibility, a biological multi-dimensional configuration, might well exist in either this or another universe, waiting to be found at the bottom of an interstellar Mariana Trench by an intrepid exo-biologist, just as life waits to be found in the immense cloud banks of Jupiter or beneath the incubating ice of Europa. But for now, until deep-space scouts report otherwise, it is certain to live and breathe only in the oceans of one world.

It has a single mortal enemy for it is one of the few creatures, perhaps the only one, that exists beyond the reach of man. Its solitary foe is also the stuff, the very essence, of maritime lore. The greatest clash of arms in the natural world takes place beyond the eyes of man. It is an elemental struggle, devoid of malice or cruelty, like the atavistic contest between the land and the sea, or the wind and the mountains. It is the struggle between the largest of the cephalopods and the greatest of the whales. Equally matched, the outcome is often dependent on a sheer effort of will rather than on brute strength, a test of endurance and stamina, rather than of animalistic brawn. Each protagonist leaves its mark upon the other, though there are few if any onlookers to bear witness to these ghostly, hidden scars. Homer's most epic titans are puny by comparison. It is impossible to say which is the hunter, which the hunted. The stronger spirit will prevail.

Perhaps it is just as well that these bouts of endurance, these acts of defiance and Calvary, take place beyond the reach of human eyes, eyes which have often shown a predilection for sadism. Even human guile and ingenuity, driven and compounded by commercial imperatives, cannot find a way to transpose these contests from the deep to an open air arena or circus ring.

A mariner plucked from the deck of a passing ship would face a series of horrors. First, the shock of the deep plunge, the violent immersion into the cold briny ocean, quickly followed by the realisation that his lungs have filled with air for the final time. Then the desperate efforts to escape the tightening coils. But the more he struggles, the more ensnared he becomes, as if he has fallen into quicksand. And, finally, the locking of the eyes. The mariner is more tightly bound by that gaze than he is by the rope-like tentacles; he can escape neither.

The two gazes, human and non-human, lock together and no key save death itself will ever set them apart. He can see in that other regard the unmistakable glint of intelligence, even of wisdom. Perhaps, too, some measure of compassion. In that moment before his lungs implode in a carbolic cloud of air bubbles and droplets of blood he knows his fate is irreversible. Mercifully his consciousness evaporates along with the air from his collapsed lungs, and he is dead, quite still and dead, long before he reaches the waiting beak, the cutting blade of an aquatic guillotine. Before he reaches the place of annihilation. There is something gynaecological about that single hard mandible, something in the fleshy folds that surround it, which hints at a Freudian doom. Thus he passes from master to meat within a matter of seconds, leaving his topside companions bemused by his sudden disappearance.

It cannot know that it is a thing of legend, the Kraken that pulls entire ships and their hapless crews beneath the unforgiving waves. But the stories of mariners plucked from the decks of ships, carried off as if by an invisible hand, are not legends at all. As the elusive wraith retreats back into the darkness, and you lean as far as you dare over the edge of the deck to follow its slow descent, you know you have been spared, that you have escaped summary judgement for venturing out upon the open sea.

Next time you may not be so lucky.

The Snow Bear

Each of us, as we grow older, becomes more haunted. The air around thickens with revenants, with the clustering, unavoidable spectres of regret. Each of these shadows has its origins in the past; each exists because at some point in our life, when our past was still our present, we weren't brave enough, or kind enough or resolute enough. We all have our Jacob Marleys' to contend with and not all take human form.

The ghost which haunts me most is ursine in nature, the most fearsome of all the bears. Or, at least, it should have been, had that fearsomeness – its most elemental quality – been allowed to roam free. It is not enough to say that he was caged in less enlightened times, for times – from that day to this – have changed very little.

I knew when I first saw him as a child that something was very wrong. No animal was meant to move like that, to pace back and forth, clearly in distress, clearly suffering. His immense cone-shaped head moved from side to side as he paced, as if trying to shake free something that had become embedded in his skull. Only

66

later did I realise that he was trying to shake free the notion of his captivity, as if it was a thorn that had become stuck in his mind, a barb that might set him free if only he could dislodge it from his thoughts.

It wasn't just the climate that clearly bothered him: the sun from which he had little or no protection and whose penetrating rays must have fallen upon him as if upon the skin of Nosferatu, wounding and corroding like acid. Worse still must have been the sullen relentless rain, drowning any capacity he might still have retained for hope, as if he had been made to wear a water-logged cloak forever draped over his massive shoulders. Perhaps he could have endured all of this had it not been for the small, the oh-so-small, enclosure in which he was forced to live.

His food, I remember, was thrown to him from a bucket, from a pail of fish heads and assorted viscera, the sweepings from a fish monger's gutter. He had never been allowed to hunt for his food but had been forced instead to scavenge in the most degraded way possible. Such affronts were offered up to him on a daily basis, a regular

67

unremitting diet of insults that no human would tolerate even for a moment.

I have not in all my days since witnessed a more wretched form of misery, a misery made all the harder to bear knowing that it had been inflicted on purpose, as a result of a conscious decision in which his wishes had counted not at all.

At intervals I saw him again as I grew older and then one day he simply wasn't there any more, the enclosure empty and abandoned, its walls no longer restricting and foreshortening the gaze which had once fallen upon them with such baleful sadness. It wasn't unhappiness that I felt at his absence but relief. And a sense of personal and abiding shame knowing that, in my visits to the zoo, I had contributed to his confinement.

The end of his days must have been yet more wretched than the tally which preceded it. Did a single bullet end the multiplicity of those days in which he had not known, from the first to the last, a single moment of freedom? Or did he pad back and forth from infancy to old age until he could no longer walk, collapsing at last under the weight of his isolation, crushed as if at the bottom of the ocean he had dreamt of swimming in for so long, his body prostrate on the sea floor he had never glimpsed.

When his eyes dimmed for the last time I hope he took with him into that unrelenting darkness an image not of his concrete, algae-stained cell but of the bright polar tundra, of the sea ice over which he should have hunted, and of the sun that would have wrapped him in its warmth, for all its distance from the Earth. I hope his dying brain gave him at least a glimpse of the life that should have been his for twenty years or more, and which his captors denied him. I hope he glimpsed a world as alien and untouched as the ice on the Jovian moons of Europa or Ganymede, worlds far beyond the reach of Man.

I am complicit in his fate, like all the others who saw his torment and did nothing about it, who saw him as just another attraction in the gaudy and tacky range of diversions on offer in the theme park, less exciting perhaps than many of the rides whose sound and fury must have added to his despair. If I am not complicit, then why does he haunt me still? Unlike Marley's business partner, I cannot lay my ghosts to rest. There can be no reclamation, no atonement. Other than to keep the promise I made to myself, on seeing his empty cage, never again to set foot inside a zoo.

*

He was born in a snow storm, his bones forged in the crucible made by the turbulent sky and the frozen ocean. And when the storm was done with him he had the strength of the wind and no small measure of its fury. Henceforth, he would always carry the storm with him, ready to discharge its turmoil and its rage when he needed to hunt or to protect himself. And the ice would always be with him too in the shape of two immense sculptured gauntlets that no other creature could match or defy.

His was a world of endless horizons, unobscured and limitless, an open domain in which he was free to travel in any direction for as far as he wished. Not even the great migratory cetaceans, who exchanged oceans as they circled the globe, roamed more freely. The only walls he ever saw were the cliffs formed by the great ice barriers, by the glaciers that flowed imperceptibly but resolutely towards the open sea. Beyond these frozen seas lay only the sky and beyond that the stars. He was a citizen of boundless space, as free as the wind.

70

He was never alone on the ice for the ocean and the sky were always with him and from time to time he shared the company of his own kind; but for the most part he was content with a companionable solitude.

And in this hollow wildness there were no wolves, real or imagined, big enough or strong enough to bring him down; indeed there are no wolves at all in these extreme elevated latitudes, no lupine-like ghosts to haunt the high castle that sits on top of the world like a vast eyrie poised above the rest of the planet.

*

His head rests on folded paws as he sleeps, not weary but content, his belly full like the well stoked engines of a locomotive, his mind dreaming, unafraid of the coming day. He sleeps beneath constellations that few human eyes ever glimpse and which somehow seem more pristine for the lack of such a regard. In his world there are no research stations, no oil rigs, no scientific shanty towns, no snow mobiles abandoned on broken treads to leak petrochemicals into the ice like poisonous wounds. The ice in his world is as unblemished as newly spun bridal satin. Each night he slept beneath a blanket of starlight,

71

shrugging off his celestial cloak when he awoke and donning in its place a mantle of snow. Thus he was camouflaged for the hunt from the moment the first photons touched the ground, arriving like soundless heralds from deep space. Their gentle, almost imperceptible impact caused the particles of ice to deliquesce and shimmer, not in a haze of heat but in a haze of cold, from which he emerged, a mirage of himself, approaching his unsuspecting quarry who doubted his very existence until it was too late to believe otherwise. Thus he goes in search of his breakfast, perhaps a bowl of stew kept warm by the blubbery hide of a seal, or salted whale meat drying on the bones of a stranded leviathan.

His mass seems to generate its own gravitational pull, drawing his food to him, as if seal and fish alike have been captured by a distortion of local space-time, falling into the pool of his mass like shooting stars trapped by a black hole. Indeed, there are times when his supper seems to throw itself onto the ice at his feet, leaping through hole and fissure, as if in recognition of the inevitability of its own fate, like an offering laid before a deity. Thus he feasts upon a well-stocked banqueting table, not upon the castoffs and leavings swept up from the gutters and drains of a slaughterhouse floor. Nor is he compelled to scavenge in dustbins and refuse sacks, to live off human waste, as some of his cousins are obliged to do.

Stretched upright on his hind legs he is tall enough to reach the heavens, to leave dusty footprints on the Moon if he chooses, or to pull the sun down from its incandescent orbit. Tall enough to overshadow anyone or anything careless or impudent enough to enter his inviolate realm.

Paw is too soft a word for the instruments of annihilation that reside at the end of his limbs. Instruments which might cut a man into three with a single pass, splicing open the flesh like a cheese wire going through the softest of camemberts, the separate pieces dissevering and sliding apart with a slippery, liquid finality, never to be re-joined. By comparison our sharpest blades are the dullest of tools.

Paws as immense as a calving block if ice released into the sea by a glacier. Just as the squalus has its fin, the rhino its horn and the sea wraith its tentacles so this bear has its paws. Behind the disembowelling scythes comes

73

the weight of the creature itself, like the rolling mass of a planet, ready to crush and devour. The claws are merely the first salvo, the first declaration of intent. His paws shake the ice as he walks, as if a crevasse might open beneath him at any moment, a gulf he would stroll over as we might a crack in the pavement. His belly rumbles as he walks, as if a volcano inhabits his chest cavity, sending ominous tremors out along his limbs to herald an imminent eruption.

In water, as on land, he is an overwhelming presence; but submerged a far more unexpected and startling sight, emerging from the polar blue waters, camouflaged by his chromatic skin. To see him swim is to be reminded of how clumsy we are in the water. He inhabits the water with a pervasive, sinuous grace like a submerged wave, as if his very bones had been shaped by the ebb and flow of tide and current.

We chop and flounder as if our limbs were ill fashioned propellers; he glides as if the ocean currents were a series of doors though which he might stroll, each opening before him on smooth, soundless hinges. He can push immense volumes of water aside with insouciant ease, as if brushing snow from his shoulders. Submerged the distance between you and he is nothing at all, no matter how far apart you might be; he will be upon you with a single sweep of his titanic arms.

It is a less than tender embrace. The best that can be said is that death would come swiftly upon the heels of such a visitation. Not even the great white shark inspires greater surprise, greater terror. Nor is there any cage that might protect you from his intentions, that might forestall the assimilation of your flesh, the licking clean of the marrow contained in your bones.

Compressed and concertinaed as in a car crash your bones would crack and splinter all at once and all together. He would pack you away as if your torso, limbs and floundering extremities were the pages of a folding book; your story would be over even as he took you to his soft but unrelenting breast and you listened to the beat of his heart, the last sound that would fall upon your ears as if from a great distance, the immense reverberations like underwater detonations. His heart like the sound of distant artillery, booming even as the puny mechanism within your own chest expired beneath the barrage.

Sheer terror might render your passing more bearable. But then again it may not, in which case the bear will smother you in his already drowned pelt, asphyxiating you twice, once beneath the surface of the ocean, and once beneath a sea of fur. It would be a good way to die, a meaningful death. And if a hundred such deaths were needed to keep the bear alive for even a single day it would be a more than fair exchange. Better that than the other way around. For there will come a time when he is the last of his kind. And when that day comes he will be worth more than all the art treasures hoarded away in every gallery and museum on the entire planet.

And if he doesn't drown you in the ocean he will smother you on the land. He will aim the black jewels of his unwavering regard in your direction and invite you to step into the long cool tunnel of his unflinching gaze, to dine with him in a cave made of ice. And if he makes a well-earned dinner of your bones, crunching your mineral essence to dust as if you had never been, then so much the better. Such a deserving feast would mean that the compliment could never be repaid, that his flesh is safe, and that his skin would remain his alone to wear.

It would be a travesty to adorn that flesh with armour, to embroil him in human conflicts fought beneath the eldritch glow cast by the Northern Lights. Worse still to see his skin draped over the anorexic bones of a fashionista, parading her vanity in the guise of a withered human being.

In our winter gardens and parks we should be building snow bears but in our vanity we see only ourselves in the possibilities provided by the snow. But how much better to construct the very creature who is snow incarnate, who wears the white distillation of his climate as if these were his garments of choice, selected each morning as if from the transdimensional wardrobe whose rear panels open onto the kingdom of the White Queen. And throwing not snow balls but snow fish and snow seals to slide down ursine throats into voluptuously hollow stomachs.

He is as much a creature of the ocean as the whale or the dolphin, inhabiting both its frozen and its liquid dimensions. His lungs exhale a mist that will, in sufficient quantity and in time, become a sea fog; and his veins are filled with the blue waters of a melted glacier. Salt crystals glisten on his fur and his ears ring with the cry of the deep-water albatross. His voice is that of the sea at its most elemental, the crashing and desolate reverberation of a rogue wave rising and falling upon itself far out in the unseen heart of the ocean, endlessly repeating its thunderous harmonics like an oceanic landslide.

He belongs to the sea as much as the ancient cetaceans whose gliding presence he can often detect beneath the ice, their immense swollen hearts like beacons for his restless hunger. Gazing at these vast submarine shadows, he often yearns to swim with them, as the leopard yearns to be amongst the antelope; but even if the ice had not kept them apart, he knows they are too big for him to bring down, that they exist beyond the reach of even his wide, devouring embrace.

Now more than ever he is a creature of the open ocean, compelled to make epic journeys in pursuit of the ever shrinking pack ice, endeavours that call to mind the great open boat journeys made by Ernest Shackleton, desperate forays into the unforgiving heart of a maelstrom in the uncertain hope of a distant landfall.

*

The ghost shook his chains at me not long ago via a story in the media: the trafficking of humans but also of an unexpected cargo: there in the back of the lorry was a cage and in the cage an arctic bear, on its haunches for the cage was too small for it to stand upright. Fear and bewilderment were evident in its eyes, just as they were in the eyes of the humans it had shared the lorry with. But for all the restrictions imposed upon them the humans were free, not confined to a cell. Whatever fate awaited the bear, it could scarcely have involved an improvement in his condition. Like his travelling companions he was no more than a commodity, an item to be exchanged for money on arrival at his destination. Looking at the image something turned over inside me, as if Marley's chains had slithered down my throat and were wrapping themselves about my viscera with all the determination of an Amazonian constrictor.

At that moment I had never felt so ashamed to be human.

The Watering Hole

Even more than the mud wallow, his favourite place is the watering hole. The open savannah sometimes dulls his senses, the weight of the sun's energy a tangible presence on his back. In this part of the world, which seems to have its own special pact with the sun, it is a freight that all living creatures have to bear, instilling a drowsiness that is often difficult to resist. It is a burden which the small oasis did much to ease, and it is always here that he felt most alive. Even though he is only six months old there is no other creature brave or foolhardy enough to threaten him, especially with his mother by his side. His proud lineage pre-dates the first human footprints and tentative camp fires; he belongs to a younger Earth. The other animals that also gather at the watering place seem to sense this. They are wary and respectful.

He seems almost to be made from clay, and there is something terrible about his vulnerability, as though he has left the womb too soon. He seems unfinished, pushed too soon into a world that means him nothing but harm.

He dips his head to drink, and the ancient light of Earth's oldest continent falls upon the single emblematic tusk, glinting as if upon the edge of a blade. It is the most fearsome weapon in nature, even more cataclysmic in its consequences than the bite of a great white shark; yet it is seldom used in anger for it belongs to a grazer rather than to a hunter. Despite his formidable mantle – the thick tectonics that shield every inch of his body – his eyes still contain the innocence of the calf, and he knows he is safe within the inviolate pentangle of his mother's protection, within the space that no one else dares to enter.

*

Eventually the tusk becomes more terrible still and he comes to the waterhole on his own, for he is now fully finished having attained fearsome maturity, a maturity that often escapes many of his kind. His gaze is more wary and more circumspect for he knows that there is one animal he needs to fear. So, even as he drinks, he listens for the thump, thump, thump of helicopter blades, for the wheels of jeep and lorry skidding in the dirt and the dust; and above all for the footfall of his relentless, stalking adversary. They have already taken his mother, dragging

81

her body behind their machines like Hector – slain and blooded and broken – paraded behind the chariot of Achilles before the walls of Troy. His eyes have witnessed their savagery, have seen how – eager and lustful – they cut his mother while she was still alive, inflicting a wound more intimate than any genital circumcision.

Once he was many, like the bison and the bear. But then came the age of industry, of the factory and the mill and the slaughterhouse. The age of mechanised weapons. And the sporting safari with its predictable and entirely unsporting outcome. We see only the bullish bulk, the well-stocked storehouses of muscle and sinew, and above these the great plates of armour more dense than a fortress wall; and most of all we see the phalanx of tightly bound hair like a perpetually drawn sword. We see, or miss-see, a brutish animal, a tank that tramples and trammels, and charges at the slightest provocation.

"*He is doomed,*" opines the lazy academic, too fat for his armchair, "*because he is worth more dead than alive.*"

"He is too expensive to save," claims the artful politician, *"we have more deserving causes. It is a question of priorities."*

So too late the armed guards and the enclosure with its watchtowers and electrified fences. Too late the funding and the special measures. Soon he will belong to the ages, to myth and legend, and to childhood story books. Future generations will scarcely believe that his kind ever walked the Earth in recent times. Like the mammoth he will be a near contemporary, close at hand but always out of reach. The same scientists who ignored him while he was alive will dream of resurrecting his DNA, swirling in their test tubes a potent brew that will not only resurrect the dead but also breathe new life into their mediocre careers.

His footfall is that of the brontosaurus, his stentorian breath that of the stegosaurus. He is both unicorn and triceratops. Yet the eyes of those searching for a lost world never seem to notice him. But other eyes do. He stands his ground when the poachers come for him, alone and very much afraid, but even the overlapping plates of his armour – which should have rendered him invincible – cannot deflect the bullets. Millennia of evolution are brought to a halt by a small projectile, by a lump of machine filed metal. Death, with its withering loss of vigour and vitality, is not the only indignity inflicted upon him. Next comes the mutilation and the maiming, the hacking and the shearing, the wrenching away of the prize. What remains is an obscenity, nature stripped of one of her finest jewels. We should weep and look away, appalled by the obscenity. But our collective gaze, inured by centuries of tribal conflict, seldom flinches.

The horn is ground down into a fine powder and traded and sold and traded again, filling the coffers of commerce and funding religious carnage. The voodoo man pours the powder into medicinal drinks that will cure nothing, while the businessman drinks an elixir that will only diminish his potency. Only the vultures benefit in the early stages of this exchange for at least they have consumed protein, feeding on a plundered and abandoned carcass left to rot beneath the sun.

At the edge of the water hole are the footprints he once made, baked into the hardened clay, like the fossilised imprint of a long vanished sauropod. He lives now in half-remembered dreams and in the spectral light of the cinematograph. The unicorned creature of fire-lit cave paintings. The rhino we might once have saved.

The Winnowing

Over time the men came again and again to the ancient oak. First they took its major limbs, its boughs and its branches. Then they took its buds and its leaves and its twigs, snapping the twigs as if they were the fingers of a child. Then, as if skinning an animal, they took its bark. They came again to whittle away at its core, each truncation – each sawing, lateral incision – reducing it in height, until only a stump remained. Then they came for the stump and finally for the roots, for the subterranean limbs that reached back in time almost to the drafting of the Magna Carta. They came till there was nothing left but sawdust on the earth, and then not even that. Thus men have come again and again (on two separate continents) to the elephant herds, to reap and to whittle, until the trails and the watering holes are all but empty, till the forest has been stripped bare. Until only a few remnant herds remain.

*

An early morning mist, little more than a pale vapour, surrounds the gathering place, obscuring the circle of water from view. At first the eye believes itself to be deceived. Surely no creature this size still exists? But one by one they emerge as if drawing their very substance from the moist, smoky air. Even when it has come to terms with their size, the eye struggles to comprehend the shape of each creature. There is something atavistic about the emerging herd. Each member of the group has ears the size and shape of a pterodactyl's wings, the great vanes brushing the mist aside as they approach the watering hole. And each has a humming bird's proboscis grown to gigantic proportions, as thickly muscled as a boa constrictor. Inevitably, despite these startling distractions, the eye comes to rest on the tusks, the great horns that are barely shorter than those of a mammoth, or a narwhal. Tusks like the smooth limbs of a plane tree, extrusions crafted not by blade and chisel but by the more tender ministrations of evolution, each protuberance shaped and worked like clay.

Their hides are like tree bark. Set into the massive, raised domes of their heads are eyes that glitter with sentience, ancestral images of frozen tundra travelling along optic nerves that are connected to a brain larger than our own. That silent gaze is unflinching, as level as a rifleman's aim. These are eyes that have been forced to bear witness, that have seen countless atrocities.

They belong to a different age, to an age when they co-existed with sabre toothed predators. They do not belong on a machine world, on a world of commerce, where the village market has given way to the stock exchange. Where the bow has been replaced by the rifle.

A foot presses into the dust – the largest footprint on the planet – bringing to bear a weight that would crush a boulder. It is followed by another footfall, another imprint in the dry earth the size of a satellite dish. Each footfall raises more than dust; it recalls a time of the many rather than the few, a time when mammoth and mastodon had nothing to fear from any other living creature. A time now long gone.

Each footfall is precisely timed and precisely aimed, and each strikes the ground like an arrow hitting the centre circle. A vibration builds in the ground, a tremor that passes out into the surrounding savannah. Each footfall is totemic, the great round feet shaking the earth.

They shield amongst them a solitary calf, like a phalanx of Roman soldiers protecting a tribune. In all but size, the calf is an exact copy of her protectors but yet more vulnerable. And that is their most striking feature, not their outsized anatomy, but how defenceless they are, especially the smallest of their number. The elders seem to sense this, to know that there is little safety to be had at the watering hole. So they don't linger, preferring to hide in plain sight on the open veldt, to disappear into the shimmering heat haze where they might be overlooked, or mistaken for something else, for a prize not worth a poacher's bullet. The phalanx becomes a column as they seek out a familiar trail and once their feet find the path they immediately feel safer. They know, or hope, that the path will lead them away from human eyes, from a gaze magnified by binoculars and the cross-haired lenses that sit atop a multitude of rifles. Thus into the chimera haze they go, walking as they have for generations across plain and steppe. And if anything is to save them it will be the sanctity of those paths. As has been the case for many human wayfarers throughout history, the trail is a form of sanctuary, an escape from persecution. And it is the only such route they now have.

*

Leading the herd is the calf's mother. On she comes like a locomotive, shunting slowly forwards, one resolute and precise step at a time. Trail fairing is how she roots herself in both time and place; each path is a single compass bearing, denoting a particular location on an inner map or chart by which she can navigate the vast seas of the open plains. It is an almanac which only her inner eye can see. Someday her daughter will possess the same guide.

The trail passes through her even as it rolls beneath her feet. With each stride, as her feet fall into the dust, she can feel her ancestors walking both beside her and within her, ghosts that the very dust – the transfiguring earth – brings to life. This ghost trail is marked by spectral cairns, by the accumulated bones of those who have been slain, and of late more have been slain than have succumbed to the slow decay of time. Some of the cairns are very small indeed, denoting the loss of infants. Her path is a trail of tears, a song-line of lament. Too many have gone now for it to be otherwise. But she carries on walking for to do so is an act of affirmation, a declaration of intent: she will not succumb to the long night of the hunter, to the nullity of extinction, not while she can place one foot in front of another. And besides, there is her calf to care for, and to teach. Her child must learn how to find and follow the paths if she is to survive.

Each trail is like a river finding its way around obstacles, circumventing boulder and tree, brush and bush. It is a trail which leads back in time to the very first valley of the mastodons, to their ancestral homeland. The path should lead forwards too, into the future, but that route is now clouded in uncertainty. She knows which paths lead to safety but also which lead to vegetation and to water and to shelter. She has spent a lifetime exploring the trails and her skills are the equal of any human cartographer. The mind-map is redrawn by each new generation, passed on by constant reiteration, by the re-treading of each route. Now she fears the map will fade into nothingness, that it will become a blank sheet of paper, tabula rasa. For the eyes of a different type of mapmaker have turned in her daughter's direction, one that wishes to wipe the slate clean of all life, one which belongs to a cartel of nation states and meta-corporations interested only in turning biological assets into cash.

She cannot know that for many the trail has led to captivity, to a concrete pen or a canvas tent, to a place where there can be no hope of freedom. For many of her kind it is where the road ends. In such places there are daily beatings with bull hooks, and with whips and with clubs. And there are only prison cells to live in. Her own torments are no less: having to watch the remorseless culling of the herd and to bear the constant anxiety over the fate of her calf.

*

When the poachers came, the phalanx closed ranks to protect the most vulnerable. The calf didn't see the cleaving of her mother, the way that they hacked at her legs to bring her down, then hacked again at the ivory, felling her mother the way they might have felled an oak. The ground shook when she fell, then shook again when they took her tusks. The calf looked back along the trail but saw only the wheeled machines and the men – the rogue humans – that moved between them.

No matter how fast the calf runs along the trail she will never catch up with her mother, for her mother's bones now belong to one of the ghost cairns. She will never again be able to breathe her mother's scent, or lean into her sheltering embrace, or feel the reassuring touch of her trunk. She will never again stand beside her mother, as her mother stares down the lion and the hyena. She will never again accompany her mother to the watering hole, knowing that she is safe even from the long-jawed reptiles that glide, barely visible, beneath the muddy surface. She will never again play hide and seek, running between her mother's legs.Or sleep standing beneath her mother's belly, beneath the womb that once cradled her still younger self. Even amongst the herd the calf is now alone. She will grieve for her mother and that grief will be as sharp edged, as abiding and as penetrating as any human loss. With a final look along the trail she runs into the heat haze, the shimmering air closing behind her like a door, and for now she is safe.

By any arithmetic their number must soon be zero; there must come a time when only one tree remains in the orchard. Their store of tomorrows, once plentiful, is now almost depleted, the stump of their timeline all but eviscerated. In the garden of life, theirs is a tree that will never re-grow. For the trails are all but empty now, the

93

footprints blown away on the wind. Remember the elephant, for remembering is now all we can do.

20719058R00054

Printed in Great Britain
by Amazon